Hilda Must Be Dancing

To Emma Dryden: For those times when
my words were as clumsy as a hippo
and she helped them to dance.
—K. W.

For Mark with love
—S. W.

ALADDIN PAPERBACKS
An imprint of Simon & Schuster Children's Publishing Division
1230 Avenue of the Americas, New York, NY 10020
Text copyright © 2004 by Karma Wilson
Illustrations copyright © 2004 by Suzanne Watts
All rights reserved, including the right of reproduction in whole or in part in any form.
ALADDIN PAPERBACKS and related logo are registered trademarks of Simon & Schuster, Inc.
Also available in a Margaret K. McElderry hardcover edition.
Designed by Kristin Smith
The text of this book was set in Footlight.
The illustrations for this book were rendered in Alykyds oil paint.
Manufactured in China
First Aladdin Paperbacks edition February 2008.
2 4 6 8 10 9 7 5 3 1
The Library of Congress has cataloged the hardcover edition as follows:
Wilson, Karma.
Hilda must be dancing / Karma Wilson ; illustrated by Suzanne Watts.—1st ed.
p. cm.
Summary: Hilda Hippo tries other, quieter, activities when her jungle friends are
disturbed by her dancing, but nothing else makes her happy until
Water Buffalo suggests swimming and she finds a new way to express herself.
[1. Hippopotamus—Fiction. 2. Dance—Fiction. 3. Jungle animals—Fiction. 4. Stories in rhyme.]
I. Watts, Suzanne, ill. II. Title.
PZ8.3.W6976 Hi 2004
[E]—dc21
2002151109
ISBN-13: 978-0-689-84788-2 (hc.)
ISBN-10: 0-689-84788-2 (hc.)
ISBN-13: 978-1-4169-5083-7 (pbk.)
ISBN-10: 1-4169-5083-4 (pbk.)

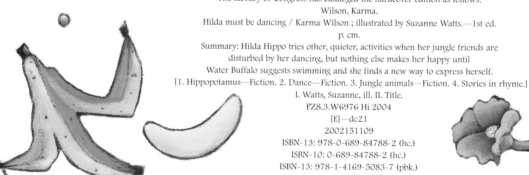
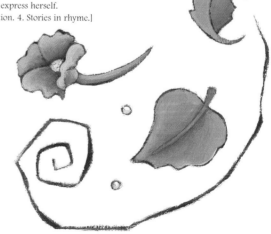

Hilda Must Be Dancing

karma wilson

ILLUSTRATED BY
suzanne watts

Aladdin Paperbacks
New York   London   Toronto   Sydney

Hilda Hippo loved to dance,
and so each day she practiced hard.
She'd twist and turn and whirl and twirl,
dressed in her favorite leotard.

She'd spin a pretty pirouette,
then leap and land on tippy-toe.

She tangoed oh-so-gracefully,
and square-danced with a do-si-do.

And while she danced in utter bliss, it sounded quite a lot like this:

KA-BUMP! KA-BUMP!
CRASH! CRASH! SMASH!

THUMPITY-BUMP!
THUMPITY-BUMP!

BOOM! BANG!
BASH!

The jungle floor would
shake and quake,
a tidal wave would
fill the lake.
Her friends would shout,

"For goodness' sake, Hilda must be dancing!"

They all hoped Hilda's hobby
was a stage that soon would pass.
But after one loud, shaky year,
they knew this phase would last . . .

and last . . .

and last.

While Hilda danced flamenco
in her favorite pair of heels,
bananas fell in gooey heaps,
shaken from their peels!

SWISHA-SWISHA

CLAP!

JUMP,

JUMP,

JUMP!

CLAP!

"Hilda must be dancing!" cried the monkeys from the trees. "Perhaps she'd take up knitting if we asked her, pretty please?"

Hilda tried to
sit and knit.
She didn't like it,
not one bit.

The yarn got tangled,
so she quit.
"I think I'll stick to dancing."

She rumbaed and she sambaed
in her favorite flowered skirt.
She skipped across the crowded plains
and kicked up clouds of dirt.

HIPPA-HIPPA

BOUNCE!

BOUNCE!

THUMP, THUMP, THUMP!

"Hilda must be dancing!"

said the rhinos in distress.
"If she'd only take up singing,
then she wouldn't make a mess!"

Hilda tried to
hum and croon,
but found she couldn't
hold a tune.

She tired of it
very soon.
"I think I'll stick to dancing!"

At the water hole she boogied
in her favorite disco pants.
She muddied up the river
and she trampled
down the plants.

SHAKA-SHAKA

BOOM!

BOOM!

BUMP,

BUMP,

BUMP!

"Hilda must be dancing!"
wailed the water buffalo.
"If she'd only take up swimming,
we might get some peace, you know?"

And so . . .

Hilda wallowed
by the shore.

She'd never felt
so grand before!
"Now, here's a hobby
I adore. . . .

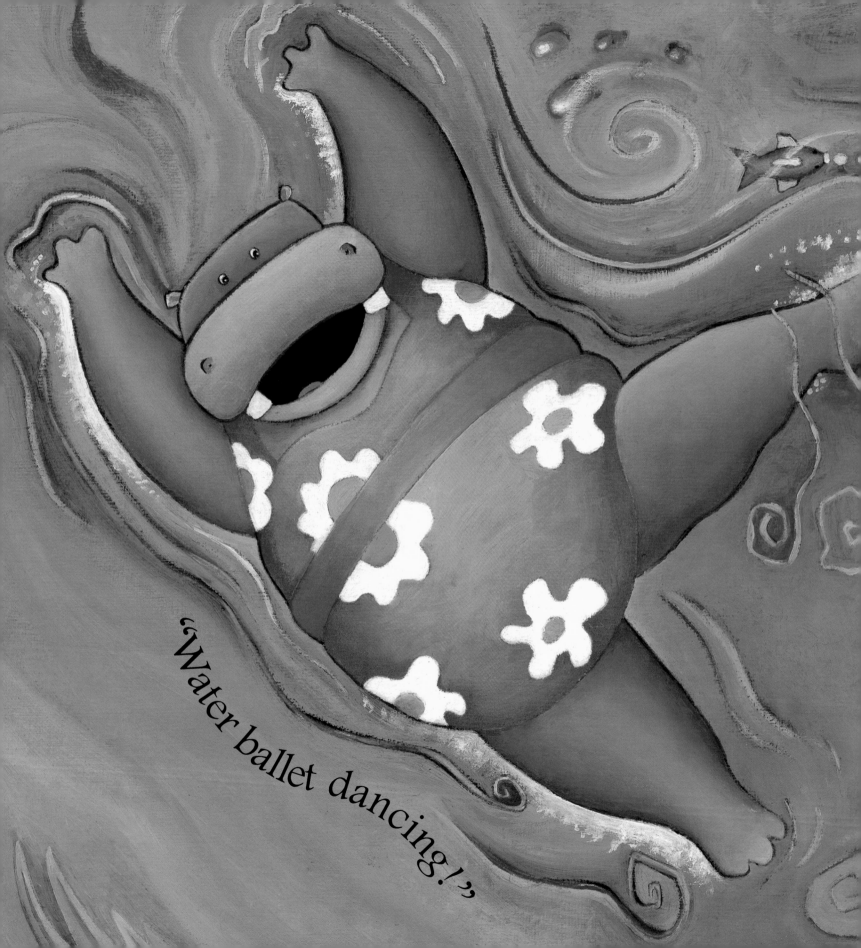

"Water ballet dancing!"

In her favorite two-piece suit
she whirled and twirled with flair.
Best of all, the ground stayed still!
She floated light as air.

And while she swam and danced in bliss,
it sounded quite a lot like this:

KER~PLOP! KER~PLOP!

PLUNK!

DUNK!

SWISH!

GLUBBITY~GLUB! GLUBBITY~GLUB!

SPLASH! SPLOOSH! SPLISH!

A big crowd gathered at the shore.
They cheered and clapped and
called for more!
Her friends cried out . . .

"Hurray!" "Encore!"

"Hilda, keep on dancing!"

And so . . . she did.